Clifford's
Day with Dad

Norman Bridwell

SCHOLASTIC INC.

New York   Toronto   London   Auckland

Sydney   Mexico City   New Delhi   Hong Kong

For Tatsuo and his dad, Tim
—N.B.

The author thanks Manny Campana for his contributions to this book.

ISBN 978-0-545-21593-0

Library of Congress Cataloging-in-Publication Data is available.

16 15 14   17 18 19

Printed in the U.S.A. 40
This edition first printing, March 2011

Whee! I'm Emily Elizabeth, and I love to swing. My father often takes me to the park. My dog, Clifford, comes along, too.

Clifford has a father, too, but his father
lives far away in the country.
Sometimes, Clifford misses his dad.

Last year on my father's birthday,
Clifford did something surprising.
He ran off in the middle of the party!

Clifford just wanted to see his dad.

He ran as fast as he could.

That's pretty fast.

When Clifford got to the country,
his dad came out to greet him.
He was so happy to see Clifford again.

Clifford's father still thinks of him as that little puppy he loved so much. He wanted to be sure that Clifford knew all the things that every dog should know.

Every dog should know how to fetch.
Clifford's dad showed him what to do
when a kid throws a stick.

Then Clifford tried it. A neighbor's dog joined the game.
The other dog got to the stick first...

...but Clifford brought it back.

Clifford's dad is a good digger.

He showed Clifford how to dig a hole.

Clifford wanted to make his dad proud of him.

Clifford dug a hole.

Clifford's dad thought it was a terrific hole.

But the neighbors didn't like it.

Clifford had to fill the hole up again.

Next, Clifford's father showed him how to look
through trash cans to find interesting stuff.

Clifford had a better way.

But the neighbors didn't like that, either.
Clifford cleaned up the mess.

Some kids were playing in a field nearby.
Clifford's dad wanted to show Clifford
how to catch a Frisbee.

The kids were throwing the Frisbee too high.

Clifford's dad couldn't catch it...

until . . .

. . . Clifford helped him a little.

Just then, a motorcycle went roaring by.
Clifford's dad doesn't like noisy motorcycles.

He started to chase it.
Clifford knew that was a bad idea!
Someone could get hurt.

Clifford raced ahead of the motorcycle.

Suddenly, the motorcycle was climbing a steep hill.

Clifford's dad caught up, but the hill was too steep for him to climb. He stopped to rest.

The big chase had a safe and happy ending.

After all that running, Clifford's dad was tired,
so Clifford gave him a ride home.
It had been a very good visit.

Clifford thought he had the world's best dad.

Clifford's dad thought he had the world's best son.

I think they were both right.